The Party Changed Everything

by
P. M. Seagrass

Cover Art by Leah Hallam

This is the future. Where scientists have made a large (and very expensive) Artificial Ring around Earth to prevent disasters, like meteors and such. A big group called the Resistance wants to stop this from happening. The Artificial Ring (Let's call it AR) also has enormous Air Conditioners to try and stop Global Warming. Oh and also the scientists live in the AR so they need constant supply drops to survive on the AR, repair it and re-contain aliens. If no supplies come, then Earth will be pretty dangerous...

CHAPTER 1

BEEPS

This is the day just before the Summer Holidays.

BEEP. BEEP. BEEP. This was the sound of Sal's very annoying alarm clock, which was supposed to be programmed to do a salmon sound. Something well known about Sal is that he really likes smoked salmon. A little known fact is that he hates plums. Very specific. Now I shall introduce the others before I go into great detail about Sal. There is Ed, who makes things like CIRCUIT CARNATION, a robot that has a built-in FLOWER APPRECIATION chip. CIRCUIT CARNATION is also a member of a group called Cyber Squad (how original, I know) which is what the characters were a part of. Finally there is Beth who likes reviews that are like teachers to bad homework, saying it "has potential". Now you finally get to read the story part.

"We might be late!" shouted a voice.

"What do you mean? School? It's online," shouted another.

"Right," the first voice replied.

This was a casual chat that Ed and Sal had on a school day. Online school was strange. Like one time Sal got an evil fish image in there.

Beth was in bed still, wondering if ice cream was a solid or a liquid. If someone disturbed her genius they would feel the pain.

"Hmmmm.... If ice-cream WAS a solid, how would you get your tongue through?"

Very IQ worthy. Very genius. Yes. Very. The great thing is that online school lets you join whenever, like the average is 9:30 but you can join at 12:30 if you were doing educational things. Like wondering if ice-cream is a solid or not.

CHAPTER 2

INTO THE METAMOBILE

The Metamobile was a low-flying spaceship. Not as expensive as your time's spaceships but very effective. It was like a private jet. Just needs to get enough speed and you're in the air.

"Wait..." said Sal, "Why isn't Beth here?"

"She isn't here?" asked Ed.

"Actually... I am," replied a voice.

"Oh."

You see, no teleporters were involved. Just camouflage. With a suit that changes to its background. The Metamobile wasn't airborne when Beth got on. Simple.

"Seen the news?" asked Beth. "Appears that a megalomaniacal money-grabbing dude called Vincent Roman is manufacturing never-before seen artificially-advanced nanotechnology."

"That is the least of my worries right now," replied Sal. "I just found a plum! A PLUM!"

"Why are we flying again?" asked CIRCUIT CARNATION, who was charged up fully.

"To go to the meeting of Cyber Squad, of course!" Said Ed.

Cyber Squad was an organisation run by kids the same age as the characters. Which is about 16.

"Ah yes... that." said Beth.

"Why do you seem displeased about going?" Asked Ed

"No reason. I thought it would get a gasp." Replied Beth.

That is some great foreshadowing right there.

"Oh, we're here!" Said Sal.

Now we can chill without constant "Are we there yet?"s.

CHAPTER 3

THE MEETING

It wasn't a meeting, they just called it that so kids could go with their parents' permission because it sounded serious. And this so-called meeting was everything but serious. There was food, competitions, more food, lasers, water, and lemonade! Oh, and even more food, with... you guessed it! AMAZINGLY IT IS MORE FOOD! So yeah. Pretty fun. CIRCUIT CARNATION can't eat anything but he participates in competitions involving, uhhhh, ummm...

Soon, when the members were heading for the exit, a face popped up on one of the screens.

"Hell-o. Hmmmmmmmmm. I am glitching. Internet connection failing. I hope you get better connection. Anyways! You guys are my workers now. Just like that. Bam!" said the man on the screen.

"LOL!" said a few members.

"Why did you say the letters L O L instead of just laughing?" asked another.

"SILENCE!" said the man.

"My name is Vincent Roman, one of the few names you will be hearing for a long time! Evil laugh!"

"Is this some special event or something? Like someone

cosplaying as Vincent Roman?" whispered Ed.

"Aren't we ahhhh, a bit OLD for that? Maybe? Or is it just me?" Said an anonymous person.

"I don't know," said CIRCUIT CARNATION.

"Well Vincent," said Beth, "I think you have a lot of potential and soon people will be hiring you for movies and you will be a very believable actor. But I'm just not buying it. Also, how big is your zoom camera? I just want to know things like that."

"I HACKED THE MEETING, NOW WORK FOR ME!" shouted Vincent.

"You are sounding desperate. Is this that thing where you want us to clean up for you? Pretty cool idea. Also this isn't a meeting. It is a party."

"WHO CARES! NOW SURRENDER!" shouted Vincent Roman, sounding extremely angry.

"Fine. We will clean up for you."

"NO! I WANT YOU TO BE A WORKER IN MY FACTORY!" shouted Vincent.

Sal stuffed some salmon in his mouth. Beth quietly collected rations.

CHAPTER 4

TRAPPED

Vincent's factory was not super beautiful but it did have jet black walls and a glass roof, which can look nice.

They were put to work straight away in the underground assembly line. The room was dark and, in some places, damp. They made a mental note not to go near those parts.

"What do we need to do?" asked Ed.

"Make stuff," Vincent replied.

"What stuff?"

"Nanobots."

"How?"

"Ok, fine. I will tell you. So first we need a motherboard, then a-"

Vincent's voice trailed away, leaving the workers bored out of their minds. Finally, Vincent's lecture of how to make nanobots was over.

"Did anyone catch that?" Asked Vincent.

"Um...it just sounded like blah blah blah to us," said some random person.

Vincent made noises that sounded like "ARGHWHYDONTYOULISTENTOME?!" and threw up his hands in exasperation.

"Ok. No guidance. Oh no no. You had your chance. Make them on your own. I don't care," Vincent said.

"Alright," the group of freshly kidnapped workers shouted in unison.

"But," Beth shouted, "CIRCUIT CARNATION is not human. Does he still have to work?"

"Oh yes. They can look up how to manufacture nanotechnology. And tell you how," Vincent smiled.

"Nice. Thank you CIRCUIT CARNATION," said the crowd forming around him.

"Bad news," CIRCUIT CARNATION whispered, "My AI is telling me manufacturing nanotechnology is illegal. And illegal stuff doesn't have tutorials."

"Oh," the crowd whispered weakly.

"Why?! WHY?! Is it because they are inhale-able?"

"Oooh. Looks like you will have to figure it out yourself..." screamed Vincent.

"This is inefficient, you know!" shouted a couple of people.

Soon the crowd parted, each worker heading towards the assembly line, not a clue how to make anything.
"Sigh..."

"Are you saying sigh instead of actually sighing?"

"Yes."

Let me tell you some attempts of making nanotechnology. There was a square one, triangle, pentagon and one that looked like a tooth. These all didn't work, if you were wondering.

"I think... after what torture we have been through... it is finally time to revolt," said Sal.

"Dude, we've just been here for 3 hours!" replied Beth.

"But we SHOULD still revolt, right?" asked a very hopeful Sal.

"Ok, fine. EVERYONE!" Beth screeched.

"Yes?" asked everyone.

"Today is the day that we gain freedom! And break out of here, and show this Vincent Roman what we can do!" screamed Beth.

A mumble of approval came from the crowd.

"Sooo... You agree?" asked Beth, a little less loud.

"Yes," replied everybody.

"Nice. So, I got CIRCUIT CARNATION to tell me the whereabouts of this factory. It appears that there is a vent with a few screws loose. If we use a metal beam as a battering ram, we can then use the assembly tables to get up there!"

"But what's on the other side?" asked the crowd.

"The control room. It needs a cold atmosphere or else it will initiate self-destruct. And if it goes into self-destruct that means all objects and machinery will not work. Any devices on the factory's WiFi will go into immediate shutdown until a new WiFi source is available," explained CIRCUIT CARNATION.

"Oh no. I was texting my little sister at home a simple re-telling of what has happened," said some random person.

"We will go after you finish texting the re-telling," said Beth.

5 MINUTES LATER...

"Ok, done!" said the random person happily, "I told her not to tell Mum or Dad, or get involved."

"That's not great. You could've told them to call the police," said Beth unhappily.

"Vincent Roman could just take their weapons and make them workers here. I'm not getting others involved," the random person replied.

"You can't argue with her statement," CIRCUIT CARNATION told Beth.

"OH YES I CAN-" Said Beth.

The next few seconds were an epic debate.

CHAPTER 5

A WORKER'S REVOLT

"Where is Vincent? He could be in the power room. He might have overheard your screaming," Sal told Beth as they crawled through the vents.

"Maybe..." Beth considered this.

After 12-20 minutes of crawling the large group of teenagers finally made it to the power room.

"Bigger than I expected. Thought it would be the size of my kitchen which, by the way, can only fit one person in it. And that is my pet cat. That's how small it is," Beth said.

"Ok, Ok, no need to tell us," Sal told her.

"CC, how do we shut down the power source?"

"A password," CIRCUIT CARNATION replied.

(If you didn't know, CC stood for CIRCUIT CARNATION. I am going to call him that now, since it's less effort. You've probably done that at school, so can't blame me!)

"Ok. What would a cunning megalomaniacal criminal genius use as a password?" Beth wondered.

"123?" Sal asked.

"No no no. That's too easy," Beth told him.

"Maybe that's what he'd want you to think," Sal argued.

"Ok, I will try it."

Surprisingly it worked.

"Turns out this so-called genius is not what he's cracked up to be," Beth said.

"Now, to de-activate it..."

"The battery is running low, better do this quick," Sal told her.

"Really? You need to charge this thing?" Ed asked. Beth saw a 10 in the battery turning into a 9.5 slowly.

"Wait a second... That isn't a battery! That's a timer! Vincent obviously knows how to use this, so anyone who spends time figuring how to use it must be someone trying to shut down the systems! Then when it runs out, he will be alerted to this area!" Beth screamed.

"Well excuuuuse me princess, I didn't understand a word of that," said Sal.

CHAPTER 6

SHUTDOWN

"Ok, quicker, chop chop!" said Sal anxiously.

"That isn't helping!!!" Beth screamed.

"The timer is running out! 5 percent, 4 and a half percent..." Ed told Beth.

"Done!" Beth told the crowd. With 0.5 percent left, Beth did it. There was a loud BRRR as all machines went into shutdown. They could hear Vincent's angry shouting as his machinery stopped working.

"Yes!" The crowd said quietly not to lure Vincent over to the area.

"I miss my cats," said somebody.

"I miss my cat too, but we need to keep moving!" Beth told them. This led the gang into a quiet chat about their cats. Eventually, Beth spoke up.

"Where to next, CC?"

"To the Living Quarters!" he replied.

"Seriously?" Beth asked.

"Yes, seriously," CC told her.

14

"Ok, to chill?" said the crowd hopefully.

"Yes!"

"My legs are happy now!" shouted Ed excitedly.

With that final victory speech the crowd moved on towards the vents.

"The vents are a very complex maze. The only way we got in the power room was by following CC's directions. Now lead the way to the sofa, CC!" Beth told the crowd.

About 10-20 minutes later...

"We are finally here! Time to rest my legs!" shouted the crowd.

CHAPTER 7

CHILL TIMES

As you may imagine this is just the teenagers getting a well-earned rest.

I will take this as an opportunity to tell you what Vincent is doing. Vincent was having a very un-chill time.

"AAAAAAAAAAAAAAAAAAAAAAAAAAAAAA AAAAAAAAAAAAAH! My lovely nuclear power source has been disabled. Must be those pesky workers. I knew they'd be trouble. Must turn the power on again," Vincent screamed.

Remember that the power source was due to explode and it hasn't happened yet? Well, if someone turns the power on again, then it will have power. Power to self-destruct. You can see where this is going.

BOOM!

"ARGH!"

Now, let's go back to the Living Quarters.

"Did anyone hear that? Sounded like Vincent screaming at an explosion," asked CC.

"Oh... The power control panel. The one that was due to explode..." answered Ed.

"Nice," said Beth.

Vincent's screams echoed through the grey hallway, advancing with each yell.

"RAGHRGH!!!"

"Hide under the covers!" Beth told them.

So they did.

"I know you are here! I am tired of playing games with you!" Vincent screeched.

"A bit of a dehydrated pickle we're in..." whispered CC.

CHAPTER 8

ASTROTECHNOLOGY (???)

"On the count of three, we make a run for the astrotechnology room," said CC.

"I'm thirsty from all this running." Ed said, as he drank a lot of water from leftover supplies from the party.

"3...2...1...RUN FOR IT!!!" CC shouted quickly.

The entire crowd jumped and ran, so quick Vincent was lost in a tsunami of running teenagers.

"Help-" Vincent tried to say but was knocked out by the sheer force of the human wave. By the time he regained the space to stand, the tidal waves of teens were long gone. He decided to just sit on the sofa and relax for a while with a hot chocolate while watching the news. The news said: "A mass kidnapping happened around the location of the annual teenage meeting of Cyber Squad. All the teenagers who attended now have been missing for 3 days. A search party has been sent but no sign of the teenagers so far."

Vincent switched it off. "Great," he muttered.

"Soo...how do we use the rocket?"

"Please, Sal. It's a spaceship. Two very different things,"

Beth told Sal.

"They aren't THAT differen-" then Sal was cut off.

"They are very different," Beth told him once more.

With that, they all went into the spaceship/rocket.

"So. I think that we need to activate the launch protocol, which requires extreme patience. If Vincent comes I will need some of you guys to distract him. Riddling talk works. Ask him what can make life, build universes, can devour all life and destroy universes. The answer is 'time', by the way," CC told them.

"Stand outside the room and try to hide the fact we are operating a spaceship. I will shout 'COME' to you. When you hear that, run for the spaceship doors and close them behind you."

"Roger that," a few teenagers told him.

"Positions! Vincent is coming," CC whispered.

The Riddling Teens were in position, they just had to wait until CC had finished activating the launch protocol.

"Aha! There you are, you pesky kids! Now back to work," Vincent shouted happily.

"What can make life, create universes, devours life and can destroy universes?" said the Riddling Teens.

"Don't tell me… an author?" Vincent asked.

"Incorrect," they said, "The answer is 'time'."

"I should've guessed that! AAAAAAAAAAAAAAAAAAAAAAA. Much anger. Much frustrate. " Vincent said unhappily.

CC inhaled (as much as a robot can inhale) and managed to somehow spit out "CoOOOOOOooooommmmmmmmmmeeeeeeee."

The Riddling Teens (as I call them) made a run for it and closed the airlock behind them, leaving a very angry Vincent saying outside the window.

"I will get you!"

They didn't care, as the ship was now airborne.

"Victory!" screamed Sal.

"Not yet, Sal. We need to get back home," said Beth.

"I know, but let's chill until then," replied Sal.

CHAPTER 9

INTO THE COSMOS

They found space suits but there were too many people so not all of them had space suits. But something there was enough of was gas tanks connected to the mouth part of goggles.

"Now we shall do cool stuff," said Beth, "Like fighting sea aliens."

"BRLARGLARGLE," said one of the riddling teens.
"Sorry, GHRAGHL. Not fighting you," Beth reassured him.
With this, the gang made it to another spaceship/rocket. It was all black with a glass roof.

"AAAAAAAAAAAAAAAARGH! This is Vincent's design. Black with a glass roof. He's out to re-capture us," Beth screamed.

"CREW MEMBERS OF THE COSMO NAUTILUS PLEASE SURRENDER IMMEDIATELY," said a robotic voice.

"NO!" said the crew of the Cosmo Nautilus.

"CREW MEMBERS OF THE COSMO NAUTILUS PLEASE SURRENDER IMMEDIATELY," it repeated.

"Oh, it's just an AI. Programmed to repeat an order until followed," said Ed.

As the AI's spaceship started advancing towards them, a corridor reached out to the Cosmo Nautilus airlock.

"They expect us to enter their spaceship through there," Beth told them, "So they are making it so we don't die from lack of breathable air. That's why it has a roof and has no gaps."

With that, an AI forced the Cosmo Nautilus crew into their spaceship.

It slapped a number plate on all of them (it took ten minutes)
"PLEASE ENTER THE HOLDING CONTAINER WITH YOUR NUMBER ON IT," said the AI.

"What is this, sleepover in a mansion but we have different rooms?" Sal said.

"Time to do nothing but sleep!" said everyone else.

"I suppose, Sal. Just not as nice," said Ed.

So each crew member either had to share a room with 3 people, 2 people or even 7. This was because of the news. The club's name was told on the news. This is because Cyber Squad is one of the most popular clubs in the city. Which means that there were... 472 teenagers attending. So yeah.

"This is uncomfortable. I am giving this abduction -5 out of ten," said Sal unhappily.

"Wait, that's illegal-" Beth told him.

"Hmmmm. I'm wondering about that water chute. How deep is it? Is it truly used for drinking?" CC wondered.

"Stay away from it CC," Ed told him, "It might short-circuit you."

"Wait! We brought the swimming equipment. We could swim through the water chute!" Beth realised.

So she shouted to all the other teenagers to put on swimming equipment (apart from CC) and then swim into the water chute.

"Don't worry CC," said Ed, "we will free you after."
"It appears that this is a long journey to Vincent's factory. There is a water dispenser in the main control room. Like a coffee one. Just pour ridiculously large amounts in. There is quite a lot already in there. We need to find the tube leading to the control room in a maze with over a dozen other tubes," CC told him.

Then the entire crowd put on the equipment and jumped in.

"How are we supposed to talk to each other?" gurgled Beth as she was underwater.

As you can imagine, nobody heard Beth say that.

She found Ed, who was following the hologram map CC showed him (robots can do that, apparently) on the surface. When he found her, he pointed to where the tube leading to the power room was. Beth got her tape and marked where the exit was. She would go back to lead other teenagers to the exit.

20 MINUTES LATER...

"All done!" said Beth after all the teenagers had been escorted to the main control room.

"Er... how do we use this?" said a couple crew members looking at the panel, "And what do we use it for?"

Beth smiled. "Make the robots dance, of course!" How random.

Soon the robots were doing the jitterbug.

"Ok, go on Ooogle maps to figure out where Manchester is. We don't want to crash into the factory again," said Beth.

There was a slight 'Cralunk!'

"Oh no."

CHAPTER 10

BA-BOOM

BANG!

"AAARGH!" said all of the crew members.

The power overload had made a massive explosion in the ship's jet booster.

"TO THE ESCAPE PODS!!!" Beth screamed like you would if your life was in danger.

All of the teenagers scrambled to get in. They all closed the doors behind them.

"Ok, we are safe now," said Beth.

The escape pods ejected themselves from the main ship. As they glided away they noticed a beeping grenade. It exploded leaving the ship as a mass of debris.

"I wasn't fond of that ship anyway," said Ed.

IN VINCENT'S FACTORY

"What? I've just read that the ship that was supposed to take my workers back has exploded," said a very confused Vincent.

BACK IN THE ESCAPE PODS

"Wow. What a brush with death, am I right?" said Ed.

As you can imagine, their troubles were far from over. They STILL needed to get home. And I'm pretty sure escape pods don't have Ooogle Maps.

"Hmmm… Where are we headed, CC?" said Ed.

"If we were gliding at Earth and we stayed in this line, we would be headed for Canada," replied CC.

"Oh. We aren't even headed for Earth? And if we were, we would be gliding to Canada?" asked Ed.

"Correct," said CC.

Soon they had drifted near an asteroid belt that was turned into a mining facility to unearth Nitrotanium, a very strong and expensive metal. It was also a shelter for miners.

"Ah yes, finally, a new place to stay. More space to escape Sal's rage about finding a plum," said CC happily.

As they found a room they realised they could just walk in. In the room was: a Mega 321TV flat-screen, a large water supply, a large food supply, a SUPABED bed and a big sofa.

"Oooh, avocados!" said Ed. The room was bright white with pulsing blue trimming and a very big window. Of course, the crowd needed to share rooms, and they also shared pods, if you were wondering.

"Hey. You're not allowed in there. That's avocado storage," said a very grumpy voice.

"Does it look like we even care?" said CC, "You are part of a Noxian settlement, are you not? Noxians are very… How can I say this kindly… Very, very dumb. Can't figure out that forks and sockets are very deadly when put together."

"You've just insulted my entire race of people. But you're right," the Noxian replied.

"Wait," said Beth, "I need to post this on the YooToob. The legendary YooToob. The one and only. Title: OMG WE FOUND ALIEN!!!!111. Video: Us talking to an alien. Editor: Sal."

"But I have no idea how editing works-" Sal protested.

"You will edit!" Beth told him.

"Also, are there actual 1s in the title?" Sal asked.

"Yes!"

Soon after the video had been posted (and quite badly edited by Sal) everyone broke out into dance, for some reason. Maybe it was because the video got 500M views from it and they now have enough money to live in a mansion in Las Vegas? Nah. It's probably that they got a PIZZA from the menu!

"This place is the BEST!!!" Sal screamed joyfully.

"Ahem… You are supposed to leave now," said the grumpy Noxian.

Pop! Pop! Pop!

27

"Wha? Pop?" said a confused Sal.

"Oh, I'm just seeing a video of bubble wrap," Beth smiled.

"Wow. Now I'll never look at bubble wrap in the same way again," said an amazed Ed.

"Oh. On the video we made there are some negative comments. Like 'Ew', 'yuck' and stuff like that. But someone called YourAverageTrombone has replied to those comments and is fiercely defending the video. That's a plus," said Beth solemnly.

"YOU ARE SUPPOSED TO HAVE LEFT BY NOW!" screamed the enraged Noxian.

"Aight imma head out," said Ed.

"YOU BETTER!" screamed the Noxian.

"Ayo, where are our escape pods? We can't leave without them," said Peter.

"JUST TAKE THESE MINING SHIPS AND LEAVE!" said a sort-of happy Noxian. He was slightly happy because they were leaving. Also not happy because Noxians are just like that.

"Ok," said everyone.

"Let me just do something..." said the increasingly suspicious Noxian.

The Noxian had turned the auto-pilot to crash them into

the dystopian planet, Equinox! Equinox has people, but they were mostly junk cyborgs who fended off evil mutant monsters day in and day out.

They used to have a 3 billion population until 97% of all Equinoxians had been wiped out due to a massive storm and the remaining 3% struggled in the harsh, icy climates and the boiling hot deserts.

"Oh look, someone got an apple tree at the party," said Beth happily, "And it's from InstaGrow! That's where my dad goes to buy plants!"

"Bye! Have fun on Equinox!" said a delighted Noxian.

"All because we just angered you?!" shouted Beth. They couldn't hear the answer because they were about 1 kilometre away from him, but it sounded like "Yes!"

CHAPTER 11

EQUINOX

"This is fine," Sal said calmly.

"You said that when we almost went into another reality just to get coffee! And I don't even like coffee!" said Ed.

"True, true. But this is different. We are going to Equonix, the theme park planet!" said a happy Sal.

"You misheard. 'Equinox', not 'Equonix'. Equinox is the one with zombies and mutant things and mosquitoes."

Sal showed very visible frustration.

"It's good I packed my bug zapper and bug vacuum," said Beth.

"How does it work?" asked Sal.

"I'll show you." She got a bit of dirt and dropped it on top of the bug zapper. It crackled and fizzled before the zapper erased it from existence.

"Wow. Can it hurt humans?" said Sal.

"No, the electricity is channelled and bugs are easy to kill or something," Beth said, "At least we can fend off mutant bugs now."

"Aren't mutant bugs way bigger? Like in the movies and also in Australia?"

"No, just a bigger taste for, um… irritating people."

"Ok."

There was a loud BANG! as the spaceship crashed into the freezing cold tundra forests known as the Ghidora Plains Gateway.

The forest was covered in ivory snow and dark oak trees which reached for the sun, shrouded by the clouds of a storm. The air was thick with unbearably cold mist.

"Brrrr....This is about as chilly as a freezer but in the sun so it needs to be even colder. Also, what is that thing?" said Sal, pointing to a large mass of fur.

"That? It's a Frostjaw. Don't poke it. Very deadly little beasts, they are. Could bite your hand off," said Beth.

"What are the odds of not getting your hand bitten off?"

"Let's see...98 divided by 89...1.101123596 out of 100."

Sal smiled. "I like those odds," he said.

"No, Sal, that's actually really stupid-"

"Everyone! I accidentally poked the Frostjaw and now let's get a sugar rush so we can escape!!!"

Everyone drank their '9x Your Daily Sugar Intake' and started running as fast as my two cats when they see tuna thinking it's for them.

"Hey! Any meat that could distract the Frostjaw for a while?" said Beth.

"I got sausage rolls!" replied Ed.

Beth threw it over to the rampaging Frostjaw and it devoured it happily.

"Awww...It rolled over!" said CC.

The mutant was actually quite like a kitten. This was turned into a "It's a kitten!" because it had started becoming smaller and smaller until it was a cute little kitten with long hair. Adorable.

"Oh, it wasn't a Frostjaw...It was a Formkitten! They turn into beasts to scare away predators and humans so they can live with their family only! It does turn into its true kitten form when a human gains its trust," said Beth.

"Sometimes, Beth, I really do think you are a walking encyclopedia," said Sal.

The small, long-haired kitten followed them until the kitten's little legs couldn't carry it anymore, so Beth carried it.

They waded through swamps and made it to the desert where the first Equinoxian town of Last Refuge was built, at which the Form kitten morphed into a Scorchpion Queen so it didn't get overheated.

"Look...An oasis!" said a relaxed Beth. Then it started

shimmering.

"NO! STAY WITH US OASIS! YOU CAN'T BE A MIRAGE!" Beth shouted. But it was too late, as it evaporated before their eyes.

After a few more mirages (An ancient temple, a village with food and water, etc.) they made it to Last Refuge.

"Is this a mirage? Because I kind of want it to be," Sal winced.

The town was about the size of 4 mansions put together and was made of rust - the reason Sal didn't like looking at it.

"Excuse me! This is a wonderful village, not a mirage!" said a lady in a leather jacket, "It's hard enough dealing with mutants like THAT!" she said, pointing at the Queen Scorchpion (The Formkitten one). "Troops, assemble!!!"

"Enemy spotted," said one of the troops. But a zombie was hiding behind them.

The zombie started infecting everyone in its path!

"Run, little Scorchpion, run!" said CC.

After they had escaped from the Last Refuge Beth had an idea.

"What if someone got a torch and shone it near one of the passing ships? They might pick us up."

"190 IQ as always, Beth," said CC.

CHAPTER 12

BGM-1065

They got a torch and waited. And waited… and waited. No sign of spaceships anywhere.

"This is boring. I need my spicy Sun Nuggets," said Ed.

"Wait! There's a spaceship coming. Get your flashlights ready!!" said an excited Beth.

The spaceship noticed them and dropped down, about 50 metres away. There was a faint "Brainsss...."

"Oh no! The zombies are gaining on us! Make a run for it!!!" said Beth.

They ran towards the spaceship, trying not to get infected. They got in and closed the door behind them.

"Phew. Just in time."

"Hello. My name is Mark Seawader. But you can call me Mark. Did you want to live on another planet?"

"YES," said Beth.

"I see."

BACK IN VINCENT'S FACTORY...

"What? THEY ARE OUT OF OUR SOLAR SYSTEM?! Guards! Scout all planets outside this solar system NOW!" said an enraged Vincent. I'll prepare a little surprise for them once they get back..."

IN THE ARTIFICIAL RING...

"CONTAINMENT BREACH. CONTAINMENT BREACH. ALL SCIENTISTS PLEASE RE-CONTAIN BGM-1065. THE WAY TO DEFEAT IT IS TO-"

The alarm was destroyed by a jet-black goopy monster known as BGM-1065. BGM-1065's tendrils ripped through the interior walls like they were paper. All re-containment efforts were useless - the creature was immune.

"EVACUATE NOW!!!" shouted the scientists, "IT CAN'T BE BEATEN!!!"

If you didn't know, BGM-1065 stood for Big Goopy Monster. The numbers are just for decoration.

"RUN!!!!"

"AAAAAAAAAHHH!"

Most scientists were fine. The others are not as fine.
BACK IN THE SPACESHIP...

The spaceship landed on an old overgrown Resistance HQ.

"What is this ship called?" said Sal.
"'Snek." replied Mark.

"Really? This massive and strong spaceship is called 'Snek'?"

"Yes. Now be quiet. I need a tennis racket. Anyone got a tennis racket?" said Mark.

"This is like a tennis racket," Beth said, pointing at the bug zapper.

"Good. There are little poison plant leaves that we need to bat away."

They ventured out into the overgrown HQ.

"Why are we doing this?" said Beth, the electric racket in her hands.

"To destroy Resistance HQ," said Mark. "Now give me that racket. Some poisonous leaves are falling in our way."

"But it's empty, and also what are they even resisting?" Said CC.

"Patience, young one," Mark replied.

Mark grabbed it but Beth didn't turn it off. Right after he made contact with the zapper and the leaves, the leaves were sent to another reality. This made him jump a bit. Then he started evaporating every leaf in his wake.

"Wow. We just wanted to have a party, now we're in space after escaping a kidnapper with a mutant shape-shifting kitten from another planet," said CC.
Soon they had reached the HQ.

"Ok, are you done setting the empty HQ on fire?" said Beth.

"Yes. Now that's done, where do you want to go?" said Mark.

"Manchester!" said everyone in a very un-harmonious voice.

"Alright," he said, before zooming at Manchester with impossibly fast speed.
You want to know where they ended up? Yes. Back in the factory.

"What a scam!" said Ed.

Then a big robot with a small glass capsule in its head walked towards them.

"Hello! Fancy seeing you so soon," said Vincent, who was in a mech suit.

A big blob of black goo fell from the sky, crushing through the roof of the factory.

"Blob. Blob blob," said the goo. Then the goo used its tendrils to smash the walls of the factory.

"Vacuum time," said Beth. She started to suck up the monumental blob but by the time she sucked it all up it had made the vacuum combust.

"Oops."

Vincent's mech started firing random stuff at the goo, but the goo just swallowed them.

"What's Vincent doing?" said Ed.

"Trying to defeat the slime. Also, my laptop is the sun now," said Beth.

"I didn't even see you bringing a laptop," said Ed.

"I just had my fifth '9x' and now I'm READY!" said Sal, "My throat is almost dissolved now!"

"Good for you," said Beth.

Meanwhile Vincent was still throwing things at the blob... a piano, a phone, a penny, some chalk. The phone didn't even get consumed by the omnipotent blob.

"Get the phone and call authorities and S.L.C.C.F. now!" said CC.

S.L.C.C.F stood for 'Stupidly Large Creature Containment Facility'.

20 minutes later the S.L.C.C.F. arrived to (hopefully) contain the slimy monster.

CHAPTER 13

THE L.M.H.

"I think that the goo is too strong so the S.L.C.C.F. called the L.M.H. unit to attack it," said Beth.

L.M.H. stood for 'Last Minute Helpers'.

"Shall we escape while Vincent is busy?" said CC.

"What did you say?" said Vincent.

Vincent stopped attacking the blob and started throwing things at the exit, blocking it.

"Why has art thou forsaken me?" said Sal.

Vincent then started attacking the blob again.

After what felt like hours the blob got a tendril into the mobility power input by ripping the wire and then thought: "Hmmm, what would happen if I were to move my trapped tendril?" which was a bad move, by the way. For Vincent and the blob.

Vincent's mecha legs stopped moving, but it was even worse for the blob. There was an agonising roar, then the blob's body was getting brighter. And brighter. Like when you look at a lightbulb and the spiral just melts together. That was what was happening to the blob. But this was no trick of the eyes. The blob was melting, and getting brighter.

After the blob's body had melted into the form of a massive ball it made a noise like the bug zapper but multiplied that by a million and added microphones set to 100 decibels!

After that the blob exploded with such force that it made Vincent's mech go flying into the factory with only one mech arm left. Vincent was fine. Thankfully, only Vincent was in the blast radius. Everyone walked towards the mech.

"It's over, Vincent. You've lost," said Beth, grabbing the phone, "Neuarin City Police, please come to City Outskirts and go to V.R. Factory as soon as possible. We have a man you need to arrest. Sooooooo, his crimes includdddddddeeeeeeeee....."

The police arrived in less than half an hour and put Vincent in handcuffs.

"Vincent Roman, your crime: Kidnapping. Your punishment: 30 years in prison," said one of the police staff.

"Noooooooooo! I'll miss my Ogniloud streak! And it was 200 days as well..."
Vincent was put in the car and was taken to Manchester's Correctional Facility For Corrupt Factory Owners (ONLY!!!)

The police also removed the objects from the exit of the factory so everyone could be free.

"Wow," said CC.
In a matter of minutes, everyone had gone home. They all hoped nothing bad would happen again for a long time...

THE END

Did you really think that would be the end? Nope. I have a NEW book in progress!

It has: Time machines, dodging things, Grapes of Wrath, leeks and garlic bread and EVEN MORE!

THE QUANTUM SPACE: SPECIAL EXTRACT

"And then, Edward The First vanished, never to be seen again," said Ed's increasingly boring teacher, Mr Bottlenose. The name describes it all.

There was only CC, Ed, Sal and Beth in online school. Mainly because everyone else was asleep.

"Ayo Sal! Want to get a SHARK IN A TOP HAT in here?!" whispered Ed.

"No, Ed. I'm planning something BIGGER."

Sal's plan was to wait until 20 people arrived and SCREAM AT ALL OF THEM. He could do this by going on the teacher's profile and pressing "Add sound" and "Add image" to make a swarm of mini Sals that scream at everyone!
"I'm never gonna give up this idea!" said Sal.

"Are you planning to scream so much everyone needs to learn sign language?" whispered Ed.

"Why, of course," said Sal.

Thank you for reading this book! I hope you liked it. Are you excited for Book 2? What's that? You want PURE, UNHINGED CHAOS in it? Well, you are in luck! I'm working on it, possibly now!

ACKNOWLEDGEMENTS

First of all, my friend LEAH who read the draft (and agreed to forget about all of it) My parents (what did you expect) and my mother's friend for thinking it was my mum who wrote it. Thank you to the teachers at my school for encouraging me. Last but not least, my cats, for sitting on my laptop all the way.

9 781916 596894